# A NOTE TO PARENTS

## Reading Aloud with Your Child

*Research shows that reading books aloud is the single most valuable support parents can provide in helping children learn to read.*

- Be a ham! The more enthusiasm you display, the more your child will enjoy the book.
- Run your finger underneath the words as you read to signal that the print carries the story.
- Leave time for examining the illustrations more closely; encourage your child to find things in the pictures.
- Invite your youngster to join in whenever there's a repeated phrase in the text.
- Link up events in the book with similar events in your child's life.
- If your child asks a question, stop and answer it. The book can be a means to learning more about your child's thoughts.

## Listening to Your Child Read Aloud

*The support of your attention and praise is absolutely crucial to your child's continuing efforts to learn to read.*

- If your child is learning to read and asks for a word, give it immediately so that the meaning of the story is not interrupted. DO NOT ask your child to sound out the word.
- On the other hand, if your child initiates the act of sounding out, don't intervene.
- If your child is reading along and makes what is called a miscue, listen for the sense of the miscue. If the word "road" is substituted for the word "street," for instance, no meaning is lost. Don't stop the reading for a correction.
- If the miscue makes no sense (for example, "horse" for "house"), ask your child to reread the sentence because you're not sure you understand what's just been read.
- Above all else, enjoy your child's growing command of print and make sure you give lots of praise. *You are your child's first teacher—and the most important one. Praise from you is critical for further risk-taking and learning.*

—Priscilla Lynch
Ph.D., New York University
Educational Consultant

For the entire Brooks clan
— J.B.

For Rick
— M.S.

Text copyright © 1992 by Joanne Barkan.
Illustrations copyright © 1992 by Maggie Swanson.
All rights reserved. Published by Scholastic Inc.
HELLO READER! is a registered trademark of Scholastic Inc.

Library of Congress Cataloging-in-Publication Data

Barkan, Joanne.
  That fat hat / by Joanne Barkan ; illustrated by Maggie Swanson.
     p.   cm. — (Hello reader)
  "Level 3."
  Summary: When Lou Lou, a individualistic cat, decides to wear a very large hat to lunch, her more conformist friend is very upset.
  ISBN 0-590-45643-1
  [1. Individuality—Fiction.   2. Cats—Fiction.   3. Hats—Fiction.]
I. Swanson, Maggie, ill.   II. Title.   III. Series.
PZ7.B25039Th     1992                                    92-7414
[E]—dc20                                                 CIP
                                                         AC

12  11  10  9  8  7  6  5                        4  5  6  7/9
                 Printed in the U.S.A.                    23
          First Scholastic printing, December 1992

# That Fat Hat

by Joanne Barkan
Illustrated by Maggie Swanson

## Hello Reader!—Level 3

SCHOLASTIC INC.

New York   Toronto   London   Auckland   Sydney

Emma opened her window
and looked outside.
"My, oh, my!" she said.
"It is a perfect day
to go out to lunch
with my best friend, Lou Lou."

Emma put on her coat.
Then she put on her favorite hat —
a very small hat.
"My, oh, my," Emma said
as she looked in the mirror.
"This is the perfect hat
for going out to lunch.
Everyone is wearing small hats
these days."

Emma patted her hat — tap tap —
and hurried outside.
She thought about lunch
as she walked to Lou Lou's house.
"It is a perfect day to have lunch
at the Lapping Cat Lunchroom.
Everyone goes to the Lapping Cat these days.
My, oh, my! Lou Lou and I can order
the Lap-It-Up Lunch.
You get a plate of yams,
bread and jams,
pepper steak, and chocolate cake.
Everyone orders the Lap-It-Up Lunch."

Emma rang Lou Lou's doorbell.
Lou Lou opened the door right away.
"I am all ready to go," she said.
"Shall we try the Lapping Cat
Lunchroom?"

Emma did not answer Lou Lou.
She just looked at her best friend.
Finally Lou Lou said, "I see
you are looking at my new hat.
I went shopping this morning.
I bought two new hats.
What do you think of this one?"

Emma did not know what to say.
She did not want to hurt Lou Lou's feelings.
At last she said, "Your hat is
big . . . and tall . . . and . . . very FAT."

"That is why I love it!" Lou Lou said.
She stepped out of her house
and shut the door behind her.
"Come on, Emma," she said.
But Emma just stood there.
"You cannot wear that fat hat
to the Lapping Cat.
Everyone else is wearing small hats."
Lou Lou tapped her foot on the ground
and said, "Posh tosh! I wear
what I like, and you should, too."

Lou Lou began walking down the street.
Emma hurried after her and called,
"You can borrow one of my small hats."
Lou Lou kept walking.

"Posh tosh," she said.

"I feel just fine in my own hat."

Emma called out again, "But everyone
will think that fat hat is silly."

Lou Lou shook her head at Emma.
"Stop thinking about everyone else,"
she said. "Think about plates of yams,
bread and jams, pepper steak,
and chocolate cake."

Emma shook her head back at Lou Lou
and said, "I cannot go into the Lapping Cat
if you wear that fat hat!"

Lou Lou answered,
"Then we will *not* go."

Lou Lou turned and began to march home.
"Lou Lou!" Emma cried,
"I am just trying to help."
But Lou Lou kept marching.
She did not even turn around
to say posh tosh.

Emma started to walk home.
"Good-bye, Lou Lou," she whispered.
"Good-bye, best friend. Good-bye,
Lap-It-Up Lunch." As she walked,
Emma heard something grumble.
It was her stomach.
"I need food right away," she said.
"I will buy some food to eat at home.
I will go to Sherman's Food Shop."

"How are you today?" Sherman asked.
Emma sighed and said, "Not so hot.
But I am still very hungry.
What do you have for lunch?"

Sherman answered, "How about
a blue cheese sandwich?"
Emma shook her head.
"No one eats blue cheese these days.
Everyone eats yellow cheese."

Sherman asked, "How about
this fine macaroni?"
Emma cried, "But everyone eats
spaghetti! With tomato sauce!"
Sherman said, "I think you should try
Margie's Snack Bar."

"Can I help you?" Margie asked.
Emma nodded. "I need some lunch."
Margie asked, "How about egg salad
on rye bread?"
Emma answered, "But everyone eats it
on whole wheat."

Margie asked, "A giant banana split?"
Emma cried, "No! Everyone gets
pineapple milk shakes these days!"
Margie said, "I think you should try
Palmer's Cookie Corner."

"Hi, Emma," Palmer said.
"You do not look so good today."
Palmer's son, Little Willy, said,
"You look terrible, Emma!"
Emma sighed. "I am starving."
Palmer pointed to a plate of cookies.
"How about a chocolate chip cookie?"
he asked. "Just out of the oven."

"Oh, dear," said Emma. "That sounds
so good, and I am so hungry.
But everyone else eats macaroons!"
"So what?" Little Willy asked.
"Suppose everyone ate doorknobs
and pillowcases. Would you?
For a hungry kitty, you are
pretty silly!"

Emma looked at the fresh cookies.
She smelled them.
She reached out and took a cookie.
She took one tiny bite.

Then she took a bigger bite.
She chewed and thought
and chewed some more.

Emma smiled. "My, oh, my!
A starving cat does not need macaroons!"

Emma paid for her cookie
and hurried back to Lou Lou's house.
Just as she got there,
Lou Lou walked out the door.
Emma called, "Lou Lou, hello!
Where are you going?"

Lou Lou said, "I am going to the Lapping Cat.
I do not want to eat at home today."
"Oh, Lou Lou," Emma said.
"I am so sorry about what I did.
May I come with you?"

Lou Lou was still a little angry.
"I am wearing my new hat," she said.
Emma answered, "Of course you are!
If I can eat chocolate chip cookies
instead of macaroons,
you can wear that fat hat!"
Then Emma looked at the hat carefully.
At last she said, "My, oh, my!
The more I look at your hat,
the more I like it. I almost wish
I had a fat hat like that."
Lou Lou said, "Just follow me."

Emma followed Lou Lou into the house.
Lou Lou took a big hatbox
out of the closet.
She lifted something out of the box.

Emma shouted, "Look at that FLAT hat!"
Lou Lou said, "Try it on."
Emma was almost afraid to take the hat.

She said, "Can *I* wear something
like that flat hat?"
Lou Lou answered, "Posh tosh!
Of course you can."

Emma put on the flat hat.
She looked in the mirror.
She turned this way and that way.
"My, oh, my! It is beautiful!" she said.
"It is delicious. It is yummy.
It is good enough to eat!"

Lou Lou laughed. "Posh tosh.
You can eat that hat,
if you like. But I am going
to get the Lap-It-Up Lunch."

Emma and Lou Lou set out
for the Lapping Cat Lunchroom.
They sang as they walked along.
"Plates of yams. Bread and jams.
Pepper steak, and chocolate cake!"
Then Emma said, "Suppose it is too late
to get the Lap-It-Up Lunch?"
Lou Lou answered, "Posh tosh!
Then we will find something even better."

Emma was surprised. "We will?"
she asked. "Really? Well, my, oh, my!"